IZZY KLINE

Has Butterflies

a novel
in small moments

beth ain

Random House ⌂ New York

Text copyright © 2017 by Beth Ain
Jacket art copyright © 2017 by Julie Morstad

Visit us on the Web!
randomhousekids.com

Educators and librarians, for a variety of teaching tools,
visit us at RHTeachersLibrarians.com

Library of Congress Cataloging-in-Publication Data
Names: Ain, Beth Levine, author.
Title: Izzy Kline has butterflies : (a novel in small moments) / by Beth Ain.
Description: First Edition. | New York : Random House, [2017] | Summary: Izzy Kline is nervous about her first day of fourth grade, and with new changes at home, there are plenty of reasons for her to feel the butterflies in her stomach.
Identifiers: LCCN 2016005017 | ISBN 978-0-399-55080-5 (hardcover) | ISBN 978-0-399-55081-2 (hardcover library binding) | ISBN 978-0-399-55082-9 (ebook)
Subjects: | CYAC: Novels in verse. | First day of school—Fiction. | Schools—Fiction.
Classification: LCC PZ7.5.A39 Iz 2017 | DDC [Fic]—dc23

Printed in the United States of America
10 9 8 7 6 5 4 3 2 1
First Edition

For my big brother,
Outener of the light,
ruler of the upstairs,
you are the walrus.

Summer Slide

While I am busy
swimming in pools and lakes,
roasting marshmallows on a stick,
singing camp songs with camp friends,
scratching the itchy bite in the middle of my back—
caterpillars are busy too.
Busy eating their way out of their cocoons
and into something else.
Something that
flutters
when I cartwheel
down the backyard hill,
when I ride my bike
down into the cul-de-sac,

skidding to a screech when the mail truck rolls up
with those cards.
Room assignments, like anyone cares which room
they happen to be in with that old,
yelling teacher and that brand-new class of kids with
only one person I used to like
for five minutes
in kindergarten.
Lilly, with two *l*'s
where there should be only one.
Used to like
until I had a playdate with her, and she cried the
whole time and told me her toys
belonged to a superhero princess from Mars,
that she was just watching the stuff for a while,
TAKING VERY SPECIAL CARE of it,
that was why she could not share it with me.
It was a good one. Lilly with two *l*'s was clever
at least.
Anyway,
there were other friends to make
and not make
that year we moved here,

all those years ago.
But last week, when the mail truck rolled up
as I rolled
down,
that's right about when the cocoon burst.
Right about when that VERY HUNGRY
caterpillar became one VERY ANGRY butterfly or
else one million butterflies.
Making me—on that last night before fourth grade—
into a night owl,
something moms say when they talk about us
to their friends.
Something they say that isn't exactly the way it is.
I am a night butterfly.
Flitting around in my bed,
in my head,
all the way until 7:25 in the morning,
when the alarm clock, whose name is Mitchell
and who isn't really an alarm clock
but who is a giant dog of the Saint Bernard variety,
licks my face.
Messy hair, rolled around and around in due to
certain BUTTERFLY PROBLEMS,

messy hair
and shorts
and a tank top.
Summer doesn't end when school starts.
Doesn't end with the reading of that
room assignment card.
Something they don't teach you at school.
You learn it on your own when it is too hot
to pretend to be nice to Lilly with two *l*'s.
Too hot to build a building out of marshmallows and
very thin pretzel sticks,
and without talking.
An activity Mom will think
sounds like loads of fun when I see her later
and when she forces me to tell her
one interesting thing about my day that does not have
to do with being hot.
The good news is the old, yelling teacher is Mrs. Soto
and she doesn't yell,
even when I laugh during the silent building of the
marshmallow buildings.
Nothing else *interesting* after that,
except for a girl named Quinn Mitchell

who stayed quiet during the marshmallow exercise
and who helped our table build a very tall,
leaning tower without my help since
I was disqualified
and she never said anything except at the end when
we/they won, when she said
no thanks to motormouth.
But she said it through a smile and also she fluttered
her eyelids,
like a butterfly,
and we all laughed because it wasn't mean,
it was funny.
And the only thing I could say back was
my dog's name is Mitchell.

Math

Ouch!

My middle finger. Yes, that one.

The finger that used to be guarded and important ever
since I learned it could curse
people.

Ever since someone else's cursed me.

Jackson.

It is on fire.

Smashed between my table and Jackson's chair,

which was flung out on purpose,

the way boys do things on purpose

without even knowing that they are doing them

on purpose.

I pull it quickly to my mouth—the cursed finger.

Kiss it? Lick it? Bite it off? What would be a good idea?

I look into the 4 sets of 2 eyes
of the FOUR ANNOYING BOYS who are staring,
waiting for me to cry
like a girl.
I bite my lip.
That's 8 eyes, I think.
Multiplication.
One math fact memorized.
If it all had to do with the staring eyes of boys
who want you to fail, math would be easier
to understand.
I think this too while not crying,
while not kicking the chair back into his table,
not kicking *him* back into his table.
Bravery, James would call it later,
under his teenager breath.
The breath that I notice so much because it is so loud—
sighing, annoyed breath.
Well, anyway, that is James's under-the-breath answer
when I say *um* a lot as I tell him
and Dad the story of my bruised finger and its
Popsicle-stick splint.
It is our night with Dad.

Our night at Dad's weird apartment,
which he hasn't decorated except for a framed
Beatles' *Magical Mystery Tour* poster on the wall
and a big stack of medical journals
on a glass coffee table
with sharp edges
that matches his own sharp edges
but nothing else.
What do you call that? I ask when I tell them how I
held in my tears with all my might.
*The same kind of thing that always happens on my night
with you,* my dad answers,
his voice edgy like the coffee table.
Dinner with a side of drama, he says.
Half smiling, half something else.
Fractions, also easier with people.
Proof of your giftedness at acting, my mom will say
tomorrow, hugging me tight
when I tell her about it.
The nurse gave me ice and a splint and said it was
okay to cry in her office.
Instead of crying I said *when will it feel better?*

Will heal one million times faster if you smile,
she said.
I'm not good at math,
I said.
They heard us laughing all the way in the front office.

Indoor Recess

I usually do not like the movies they show us
during indoor recess because they are
babyish or else they are about ogres
and I hate the whole idea of ogres.
Even Shrek.
I get why they made a movie about him, but I always
wish they would just let us color or something at
indoor recess.
Let us be.
But this was something today.
This *Free to Be . . . You and Me* video.
It was something different from the start, and not just
because there was singing and
music, which I love, but—and this is IMPORTANT—
because it was funny.

Two babies are talking in a nursery and they don't
know if they are boys or girls because
they are both bald.
That's funny.
And then there are so many other funny things,
funny characters, funny songs.
Don't dress your cat in an apron, someone says later,
because it just doesn't make any sense
to wear things that don't make any sense
for who you are.
That was the point, I think.
And then another, called "Helping,"
which isn't actually about helping at all
and which made us all laugh.
Even the boys.
And then I got the idea that this whole thing is about
LIFE LESSONS,
something Mom says in a big TV news voice she saves
only for when she's talking to me about something
important,
and she thinks important things are funny, apparently,
or that they should be funny,
which is funny.

But she's right.
I absolutely always remember the things
that made me laugh.
Like the idea that "Parents Are People,"
something they say in one of the songs,
or that women can do anything men can do.
Funny that anyone ever thought any different, I mean.
We're going to put it on—the whole fourth grade—
in a concert,
and all I want is to sing a solo.
I want to sing "When We Grow Up" because I think
it is meant to be sung
by me.
I hope no one else in the whole fourth grade can sing,
then maybe I'll have a chance.
I hope Quinn Mitchell isn't as good at singing as she
is at building things out of food.
And I hope they make a boy sing
"It's All Right to Cry."
Because that would make me laugh.
And then I would remember it forever.
That LIFE LESSON.

After-School Activities

You don't do a play in third grade or fifth grade at
Salem Ridge Elementary.
Only in fourth.
And fourth grade, as far as I can see,
is when you—ahem—*I* will be the most nervous
I will ever be.
Not third or fifth.
Because I was younger in third.
Will be older in fifth.
Less nervous.
In middle school I will like boys,
I am told
by my grandmother,
who thinks I like boys now,
the way I go on and on

about these FOUR ANNOYING BOYS in my class,
who make me want to scream, even though they can
be funny when they make farting noises
or flip their eyelids inside out.
But it is hate, not like.
I only like James, my big brother.
Quinn would like an older brother but she has an
older sister, who talks on her phone all day and night
and slams her door a lot.
I have to walk you to drama, James mutters at me
after school.
I have to be a good actress so I can get a good part in
the fourth-grade play.
Okay, I say, and I go on and on about trying to be
serious enough to get the part of Baby Girl in
Free to Be . . . You and Me.
Well, you're serious, he says, which makes me want
only to be silly.
I cross my eyes at him.
He says *why can't you hear a pterodactyl go to the
bathroom?*
Why? I say.

Because the P *is silent. The pee, get it?*

That's not a very serious-acting kind of joke, I say.

Free to Be . . . You and Me *is not a play for serious*
actors, he says.

Tell that to Marlo Thomas, I say. Marlo Thomas—
according to my music teacher,

who is new and just married and wonderful

and who used to be Miss Hall for the first six weeks

of school and is now Mrs. Johnson.

And Mr. Johnson, her new and young and just-
married husband, is the orchestra conductor—

Well, according to Mrs. Johnson, Marlo Thomas is

the writer, *the creator,*

of *Free to Be . . . You and Me.*

I know James does not know who Marlo Thomas is,

because my brother is not the type of person to know

something like this.

He knows rock bands and sports teams and—

She's the sick-kids lady, he says. *Has a famous hospital*
for sick kids.

No way, I say.

Truth, he says. *Ask Mom.*

After drama with Elana, who teaches me to sing *and*
to act, *because they are intertwined,* she says,
I call my mom at work and ask her about
Marlo Thomas's hospital.
St. Jude's, she says. *That kid and his memory,* she also
says.
She had thought James would be president one day
with that memory,
that *everything.*
When I hang up, James has gone to his room and
I know that means I can't tell him he was right.
Can't watch him stick out his pierced tongue at me
and wonder how much it hurt and what made him
do it and what it tastes like with ice cream on it, or
spaghetti, and does the spaghetti get tangled up.
Can't duck when he throws a pillow at me to
make me stop asking
SO MANY QUESTIONS!
I may not remember everything the way James does,
but I bet I will always remember
what James's pierced tongue looks like.
For the rest of my life.
Maybe James can still be president.

Maybe lots of people will vote for him
because they have been hoping
all this time someone would come along
with something as interesting
as James's tongue.

English Language Arts

Some things in Free to Be . . . You and Me *make
me think that the writers are trying to tell us
something—*
is what I would say if I were writing an essay about
Free to Be . . . You and Me
on a test, which I would not be
because that would be too interesting.
Like when—
this is a SUMMARY—
*a new kid moves in and he's worried about making
friends and all that but then he meets his neighbor,
who is a girl, and she says she has no friends either
and neither does this other kid she plays with. Well,
since we all have no friends, the new kid says, and*

we all like to play together, maybe we ought to start
a club.
That's funny, right?
I mean, they all say they have no friends but they have
each other.
That is an INFERENCE—
an inference gets extra points on a test.
Well, last year there was no Quinn.
She was in the fourth class,
and I didn't know anyone in the fourth class.
There used to be three classes until there were so
many kids,
too many kids for three teachers to handle.
So they made a fourth one, and somehow
all the kids I never knew anyway
ended up in the fourth class.
This year I am in the fourth class,
and Fiona and Sara—
the best friends I made in kindergarten, after the
playdate with superhero-princess
Lilly with two *l*'s—
are in a class together.

They only play together now,
at recess.
Only take dance together and play soccer together.
Soccer was always their thing
and not mine.
All those girls high-fiving and running so fast
in a group.
I never knew what to do or where to go
and I'm not good at losing.
Dance was my thing for five minutes
before singing became
the only thing.
That's it, THE END for everything else.
Now Fiona and Sara are in Friendship Club together,
and not a made-up friendship club,
a real one,
run by the school!
They get to skip recess once a week and do something
together.
It's like Girl Scouts, my mom said
when we got the letter.
Only I didn't know we ever got the letter.
She decided for me.

I doubt it's for you, she said later,
after I'd found out about it.
After it was too late.
I believe most things she says but
maybe not this one thing.
Everyone wants to be in a friendship club.
And I love Girl Scout cookies.
Frozen Thin Mint cookies.
I watch Fiona and Sara leave lunch a few minutes early
for Friendship Club.
And I make a CONNECTION to
Free to Be . . . You and Me,
something else you get extra points for on a test.
Didn't you get invited to join, Izzy? Sara asks me
on her way out.
I shrug because my real answer is too complicated
and because she looks so happy to be going,
whether I have been invited
officially
or not.
I turn away and say
Hey, Quinn, maybe we should start a no-friend club,
like in the play.

Maybe, she says, *if I can be president.*

She says this in a presidential voice.

Quinn's a little bossy. But she's organized and very good at pretending.

Outside of Quinn, the only organized person I know is my dad, and he is terrible at pretending.

I'm glad that Quinn is both.

I didn't think that was possible.

She can be president.

I'll be the entertainment.

Bonus points for creativity.

Substitute

When someone stands in for your real teacher,
they are the substitute or,
as we say in fourth grade,
the sub.
Sometimes—most times—it is someone terrible
who yells a lot and reads a picture book when you
are supposed to be doing something productive like
working on your Colonial Fair project.
And not a good picture book that makes you laugh
or think.
A picture book that should never have been a book
at all.
It is maybe about a kid and a dinosaur and a grandma
who doesn't look or talk
anything like a real grandma.

She has an old-fashioned hairdo and says *there, there.*
Makes you wonder what the big deal is about
writing books,
when bad books can stand in for good ones.
But today the substitute is pretty, with long hair and a
shiny engagement ring.
She asks us a lot of questions about ourselves and tells
us some things about herself.
She is thirty-four and has a yellow Lab
named George Washington.
Not George. George Washington.
As in, *Do you need to pee or poop, George Washington?*
That is what the substitute actually said.
She writes her name on the whiteboard.
Miss O'Dell.
She sounds like a character in a book.
(And not a dinosaur-and-grandma book.)
During snack, she asks me how I think she should do
her hair for her wedding,
and I suggest a wrapping side braid,
and she seems to really like that idea.
I feel excited for her wedding and wonder if I will ever
see her again, if I will ever know

how she wore her hair
in the end.
We are going to do a math marathon with another class,
you guys, she says.
A mathathon!
Mrs. Soto would not ever call us *you guys*
She would also not be excited enough about a math
marathon to call it a *mathathon.*
Mrs. Soto likes things the way they used to be—
chalkboards and colored chalk and time for a
handwriting lesson, even—
with three perfect lines, one dotted and the others
yardstick-straight—
which is why I like her.
Who doesn't like things the way they used to be?
Except a *mathathon* sounds kind of exciting,
an exciting new name for something that
used to be boring.
So boring that every time we do it, I daydream about
Jackson Allen tripping over the leg of a chair
and into a big table of tempera paint.
Because how funny would it be if he tripped and fell
into paint in front of everyone?

Pretty funny.

But things like that only happen on dumb TV shows
and inside my head during math facts.

We go to the gym.

A good place for athletic-sounding math, but we are
there for more space and not for exercise.

That's fine with me. The change of scenery is enough.

Only the scenery comes with another class.

Fiona and Sara's class.

Miss O'Dell and her sparkly ring

divide us into groups,

me with Fiona and Sara.

Quinn with Jackson Allen and Lilly with two *l*'s.

Division.

We are supposed to test each other on multiplication
facts,

which drives me crazy because I keep forgetting to
memorize them.

I get distracted at night with reading books, and my
mom quickly quizzes me on the 2s and 3s
and signs the paper and turns out the light.

Can't deal with the big ones tonight, she says, and I go
to sleep feeling guilty feelings about skipping

the big ones.

(She does not say *there, there.*)

But I am excellent at the small ones.

And especially bad at the 12s.

Every time you forget one,

the whole group does jumping jacks, Miss O'Dell says,

pulling her hair into a bun.

A bun would be a nice wedding hairdo too, I think.

Mathathon! she says for the second time, winking at me.

Her wink makes me feel something but not

less nervous

about doing math with my old friends.

Let's just do the twos and threes, Fiona says.

These are the first words Fiona has said to me all

school year,

but it doesn't seem like she knows that.

Yeah, and the elevens.

Definitely the elevens,

Sara says.

We all laugh because we all know that 11 might be

about as easy as multiplying 1s.

$11 \times 2 = 22$

$11 \times 3 = 33$

$11 \times 4 = 44$

We talk really slow so we don't run out of easy
math facts, and our slow talking makes everything
especially funny.

Eee-levvvv-uhn tiiiiiimes siiiiiiix, I say.

Siiiiixty-siiiiiiiiiiix, Sara says.

I am laughing the kind of laugh with Fiona and Sara
that I used to laugh, when things were the way they
used to be.

I look sideways and see that Quinn is zooming
through the facts and laughing with Jackson Allen
and Lilly with two *l*'s, which makes me a little bit
mad because what is so funny about Jackson Allen
except his face?

Then I feel bad.

Guilty, like I do when my mom signs the practice
sheet.

Guilty for wishing Jackson Allen would fall into paint
in front of everyone.

Guilty for hoping Mrs. Soto needs another day to
recover from whatever is wrong with her,
for liking this sub so much.

Guilty for laughing with Fiona and Sara.

Guilt, I think,
is when something feels good and bad
at the same exact time.
Slow-talking old friends substituting for fast-talking
new ones.
I need to do jumping jacks to shake off the feeling.
Let's do the twelves, I say.

Picture Day

Do you see this?
What does it look like to you?
A mountain . . . or a molehill?
You agree. It is a mountain.
No? You think it's a molehill?
You think it's a *small* bump?
A small matter of licking your hand and patting it
down and turning the bump back into
normal, patted-down hair?
You think maybe I didn't try hard enough?
Didn't ask Quinn to try?
Lilly with two *l*'s, even?
Didn't run into the smelly school bathroom and stick
my head under the sink?

Didn't squeeze paper towels filled with school sink
water directly onto the bump?
You think maybe I didn't end up having to go to the
nurse's office for mismatched
clothes on account of all the *molehill* water that had
accumulated on my BRAND-NEW picture day outfit?
It was purple, my BRAND-NEW picture day outfit.
Now it is sopping and covered in paper-towel lint.
It would have looked nice with the blue-and-white
background of the pictures my mom
ordered weeks in advance.
We chose it for that exact reason.
Because it would look just perfect with the blue-and-
white background.
You know what does not look just perfect with the
blue-and-white background?
A sweatshirt that says *Welcome to the Jungle*.
A sweatshirt that has monkeys swinging from vines on it.
A just-in-case sweatshirt someone donated to the
nurse's office *just in case* a kid with a giant wet bump
on her head needed to change into it on PICTURE DAY.
My mom ordered the A package.

Not the B package.
Not the C package.
Not the D package.
Not the E package.
The E package only has the class picture.
The A package has one million copies of the same picture.
One million copies of the same *Welcome to the Jungle*,
monkeys-swinging-from-vines,
wet-head,
giant-mountain-bump picture.
It is a mountain bump.
Unmovable by school sink water.
So you agree.
We are on the same page.
(I do not make mountains out of molehills.
It was a mountain in the first place.)
Is it good? I asked my mom early this morning
in her hurry.
It's good, Mom said.
Any bumps? I asked.
No bumps, Mom said.
Ahem.

Playground

There is a fairy tale in *Free to Be . . . You and Me*
that is nothing like
other fairy tales.
We watch it in class just before recess and it is a very
old-fashioned-looking cartoon
and not nearly as beautiful-looking as *Cinderella*.
It's kind of ugly to watch, actually, and I am
glad we won't be performing it at the end-of-year play.
We're only doing the parts with singing.
But Quinn and I cannot help acting it out
on the playground
while the boys play wall ball and while Fiona and Sara
watch them play wall ball,
when they used to play wall ball
themselves.

I am Princess Atalanta and Quinn is Young John and
they are racing—all the men in Atalanta's village are
racing her to see which one beats her.
The one who beats her gets to marry her.
In the end they tie, because Atalanta is fast and smart
and doesn't want to get married.
Doesn't want to clean the house all day and night,
waiting for some prince and an uncomfortable glass
slipper to come along.
She can fix things, Atalanta,
can even fix the race
itself,
after all.
She can't bear the idea of marrying someone who can
run fast but who maybe can't do
one other interesting thing.
But Young John is interesting and
Quinn does a very good job of having a deep
Young John voice.
Let's travel the world, Quinn says
after we pretend-race and pretend to cross
the golden finish line
in a pretend tie.

I'll go by ship, she says.
And I'll go by horse, I say in a
high-pitched princess voice.
Never mind that I am a princess who can run fast and
fix things.
I do a high-pitched princess voice anyway.
Should we talk about telescopes and pigeons?
Quinn asks.
I snort.
What? I say, laughing so hard because Quinn is still
talking in a very low Young John voice.
That's what they say, she says,
starting to laugh hard too.
I know, I say,
gasping.
They became friends! she says, practically screaming
with laughter.
Friends! I say.
We are laughing so hard for no reason except that
telescopes and pigeons are funny topics of conversation
for a princess.
They never get married in the story.
That's the point.

They go their separate ways to explore the world.
We hop onto the playground spinner
and stand face to face while it goes in circles.
Everything is blurry as we spin.
Blurry wall ball game.
Blurry old best friends.
Blurry teacher's aides yelling at
blurry kids to remember their coats.
It is time to go inside.
You're a good actress, I say to Quinn.
You too, she says.
A funny princess, she says, grabbing my hand.
Telescopes and pigeons, I say,
holding on tight,
and we laugh all over again
until Mrs. Soto shushes us back into our seats.
At the end of the cartoon fairy tale,
they say that no one is certain if Princess Atalanta and
Young John ever get married.
They say it is only certain that
they are friends
and that they are living
happily ever after.

Word Problems

Who: You!
What: Sara's Sweet Dreams Slumber Party!
When: Friday night at 7!
Where: 1 Licorice Lane
(just kidding, same old address but sweeter)
What if: Quinn isn't invited?
How: will I know if she is or she isn't?
Why: are birthday parties so stressful?

Friday Night Lights

The doorbell is a gumdrop.
There is a candy-heart path to the basement,
red licorice strings wrapped around the railing.
At the bottom of the stairs,
I plop my sleeping bag down in the
cotton candy corner!
Our sleeping bags, rolled into soft logs
and piled into a heap,
are part of the decor,
part of the game of Candy Land that has come to life
in Sara's finished basement.
Little candy-colored lights crawl up the columns,
zigzagging the ceiling into a sky of
candy-colored stars,
making their way back down again almost to the floor,

plugging in tight to the outlet
next to the snack table.
We make candy sushi out of
Swedish Fish and Rice Krispies Treats
and Fruit by the Foot.
We dance and sing and make music videos and take
big whacks at a piñata
in the shape of the boy band Sara loves so much.
So much that they replaced the puppies
on her school folders,
so much that the goody bags
have their picture on them too.
So much that Sara and Fiona are going to see them in
concert for Fiona's birthday.
So much that Sara made a giant bat out of
jumbo plastic Pixy Stix to use as our only weapon
for breaking up that boy band
piñata.
When no one can even make a dent,
Fiona grabs it and says *my turn!*
and we all cheer for her
and her power.
Even I cheer as Fiona takes the biggest whack yet

at her beloved band and still
they do not break up
but together
as a band the whole piñata
goes flying off of its licorice string
and into Sara's face. Hard.
Sara, who loves sweet things,
like puppies and candy
and boy band piñatas,
is suddenly not so sweet
herself,
kicking and hitting that candy-filled,
boy-band-shaped box
(like we even need more candy)
until things go flying,
Sara up the stairs,
lollipops and gum balls
everywhere else.
Candy Land.
Other girls, barely my friends anymore,
go about collecting the candy, and Fiona sulks.
I follow the trail, like the old game,
back up the stairs through the candy-heart path,

past the front door with the gumdrop doorbell,
until there is no path, but I know the way
to Sara's bedroom.
The bedroom where I had my first sleepover.
There is still a puppy poster above her bed,
still pictures tacked up of us in kindergarten,
at the dance recital,
at last year's end-of-year picnic.
Too much sugar, I say.
Sara smiles.
Sugar rush! we say at the same time,
remembering the time we got a sugar rush
from eating icing out of the can last year
at Fiona's birthday party.
It was an accident, I say.
I know, she says.
*That's what happens when you eat too much candy sushi
and try to beat up a boy band piñata
with a jumbo Pixy Stix bat,* I say.
Don't say I didn't warn you, I say,
shoving her shoulder with mine
till she smiles.
I wish we were still in the same class, she says.

Maybe next year, I say.
And we walk back down together,
roll out our cotton candy sleeping bags,
and fall asleep watching a movie,
the candy-colored stars lighting up the dark.

Monday Morning Quarterback

How was the party? Quinn asks,
and I don't know if I should say
what party?
or
it was all right.
You can tell me all about it, she says,
unpacking her backpack,
setting up her station nice and neat
the way she does.
I went to Benihana, she says.
Had my own party, she says.
The chef flipped a shrimp into his hat,
she says.
Made a volcano out of a stack of onion slices,
she says.

Did anyone at Sara's party make a volcano
out of a stack of onion slices? she asks,
lining up her pencils just so.
No, I say.
A volcano out of other things, I think.
What was the occasion, I ask,
sounding like my dad and not like me,
for the onion volcano?
I don't think you need an occasion
for a sliced-onion volcano, she says.
Anyway, there was a boy band piñata, I say.
I would have loved to take a swing at that, Quinn says.
And I laugh because I did think of her that night
as I swung the jumbo Pixy Stix bat.
I did think that Quinn, who doesn't love puppies
or candy,
who doesn't love boy bands either,
who loves Broadway and singer-songwriters,
like I do—
I think that Quinn would have found a way
to take down that piñata
and it would not have hit Sara in the face
and I would not have had to go into Sara's bedroom

and see that puppy poster over her bed
and remember my first sleepover.
I would have put my sleeping bag next to Quinn's
and we would have planned our tenth birthdays
together—
Benihana and sliced-onion volcanoes.
I would have loved to see that, I say.
I make a note in my homework folder:
* *buy boy band piñata for Quinn*
* *fill with onions*

Thanksgiving

Quinn has the type of parents who both show up for
the Thanksgiving feast.
And the Book Fair.
And recess sometimes.
I have asthma, she said one day,
swinging high on the swings,
higher than me,
maybe sorry her mom comes to watch sometimes.
Sorry her mom cares whether she's breathing well
or not.
I was not sorry.
I'm not sorry my mom doesn't come for the feast.
This place is full of germs.
She takes care of old people, for God's sake.
They have a feast too. The old people.

I have to go to theirs.
Maybe you'll sing something, she says
late on fourth-grade Thanksgiving feast eve.
Too late.
Too late for washing dishes and
checking math homework.
Maybe you'll sing something at mine, I say back.
Ha ha. Very funny, she says, feeling around for the
low part of her back.
I dig my fist into it for her. The small of her back.
I learned that from my dance teacher.
The dance teacher I don't see anymore,
who Fiona and Sara see three times a week still.
Thanks, babe, she says, stretching her hands out to
lean on the counter.
Formica, damn Formica, she always says,
mad at our countertops for not being marble.
We were always going to do a gorgeous kitchen, she says.
The *we* is her and my dad,
who won't be at the feast either,
who isn't the kind of dad
who comes to a classroom feast.
The faucet runs and my fist digs deeper.

Quinn's mom includes me in their family at the feast,
plopping a turkey made out of marshmallows and
Swedish Fish onto my paper dessert plate.
Cutest thing ever, she says
while she leans in between Quinn and me,
and her husband takes a picture of us smiling.
I don't eat the marshmallow turkey.
I want to show Mom.
I want to show her that I didn't eat that germy thing.
I want to sing for her old people.

Common Core

It is getting very hard
to do all this.
To concentrate so hard.
These tests.
I haven't done well on many of them.
I am not fast.
One was so long it almost killed me.
And now
my arms shake from all the work of holding
this pose.
A plank.
One minute
and counting.
Yoga is good for the core, says Mrs. Regan,
who is probably a yoga teacher in her spare time,

since she can talk
and plank
and be a gym teacher
all at the same time.
Good for Quinn for being so good
at every single one of these gym tests.
Good for physical education, my dad will say tonight,
for finally doing something to shape this country up.
I'm not giving up this time,
till I'm the last one planking.

Polar Express

Jackson Allen's pajamas look the exact same
as his clothes.
Sporty pants and a long-sleeve T-shirt, I think,
looking down at my fuzzy bottoms and
red hoodie sweatshirt.
Rolled out of bed this way,
slept in pigtail French braids
just so I wouldn't have to do my hair.
James, looking at me funny in the kitchen—
Polar Express day, I explained.
Polar Express! he said, smiling more than he's smiled
in such a long time.
I believe! he said, remembering that the book is about
still believing in things that were hard to believe
in the first place.

You do? I asked.

Yeah, right, he said.

Why do I ask? I thought.

Not that we would believe in Santa,

not that we believe in Judah and the Maccabees
either.

I definitely believe in wearing pajamas
to school.

Quinn's in red footies—FOOTIES!

And everyone is jealous because she looks so cozy

and because everything Quinn does makes everything
everyone else does look

less interesting.

The boys don't make fun of Quinn because Quinn
wouldn't care if they did.

So she wears footies and they wear sport pants and
long-sleeve T-shirts that look

less interesting
than ever.

A few days ago, Quinn and I got to spray fake snow
all over the windows of our classroom.

After that, we got to walk the halls with our
spray cans,

spraying snow on any window we could find.

It was very festive.

Fake snow smells like winter and Christmastime

the way fake butter smells like the movies.

We ran into Fiona and Sara on our way.

I was cheerful,

festive.

I was thinking we could be a group.

Hi! I said.

Let's all wear red pajamas for Polar Express, I said.

Okay, Quinn said.

I have red pajamas, Sara said.

Not me, Fiona said. *You guys do red,*

she said. *We're going to do something else.*

It is overly hot on the day we walk through the halls,

making believe we are on a train

bound for the North Pole

on the last day before Christmas break.

Hot in the winter,

hot in the summer.

Schools only have one temperature.

Unless you're on the

Polar Express!

And you walk past two girls who are not in red,
not in footies
but in sweatpants and
boy band sweatshirts they got together
at a concert
probably.
Then you might find a cool breeze,
arctic even,
I believe.

Project

In second grade I had a leaf project to do over a school
break,
and I was happy to do it, scooping up all the leaves in all
their different colors and sorting them and labeling them.
Biggest, smallest, best-smelling—hint: none of them
smell in the fall—brightest, strangest shape.
And I made a leaf creature out of maple leaves because
they look like they have arms and legs anyway.
I collected those leaves with my dad and on our walk
he said he was leaving,
that he was getting his own place.
But you have a place, I said, knowing that his place
was not here,
knowing that this place was a place that made him
quiet and angry

and always leaving and
not settled on the sofa and tickling and cheerful the way
having a place was supposed to make a dad feel.
We went on collecting leaves anyway and building
that leaf creature and I didn't cry
until the nighttime, when he wasn't there because his last
day living in our house was on the leaf-collecting day.
And now I have this map project to do and it is harder
than the leaf project and it is due
after the Christmas break,
and now I'm afraid of projects
because of what someone might tell you right
in the middle of one.
That's why I hold up my hand when James comes in
just as I'm tracing over all my pencil marks
with a Sharpie.
Don't tell me anything bad, I say, not looking up.
Mom's working late, he says. *I'm ordering in Chinese.*
Good news, I say, and I cry
right on the fresh Sharpie-inked state capital star.
For extra credit, I will add a weather pattern to my map.
A rain shower in Albany.

Punctuation

It is hard to pin down Quinn Mitchell.
She has a lot to do.
My mom and her mom have tried to get something
on the calendar,
but we both do a lot.
Singing and acting and homework;
semicolon,
and Quinn does tae kwon do a lot,
like every day.
She is a red belt.
"The overscheduled child," my mom always says,
miming actual quotation marks in the air.
When I finally go to Quinn's house, I see her belt rack
up on her wall of her room and a poster of her
high-kicking a board.

Her room looks like a page from a teenage-bedroom
catalog. Turquoise, with little white lights strung
around as if it were an outside garden party.
And pictures of one million people and places
tacked up on the walls
with colorful pushpins.
Belts and medals and certificates—
one from St. Jude's.
St. Jude's.
I can't believe it.
St. Jude's?! I say with a question mark and an
exclamation point in my voice.
The asthma. Quinn says it with a period in her voice.
Hmmm, I say. But I don't ask anything else because of
that period, and I get back to looking around—
dolls and Barbies and Kens and shoes and boots and
high heels, even.
My sister's, she says. *Try them!* she says.
I do and I almost break my ankle before I take one step,
wobbling over to the mirror to see my big feet,
almost filling them up, the strap around the heel
hanging just a little loose.

Bigfoot! Quinn says, but I can't look away.

I admire myself in the mirror.

I admire the room in the mirror too.

It is a collage of her interesting life.

Quinn puts on the radio and we try on her sister's old

dresses and pretend to go to a school dance together.

We have pretend dates, and we dance,

jumping on the bed to a fast song, then dancing

cheek to cheek for a slow one, and Quinn leads, and

then we collapse in our dresses and heels

and laugh so hard I wonder if it will ever stop.

We are a run-on sentence.

Quinn's mom knocks on the door—a hyphen—

and calls us for a snack.

We sit at counter stools and Quinn's dad calls from

work and we put him on speakerphone and he tells us

jokes and says

I love you, girls,

to his wife and his daughter before he hangs up.

I picture him sitting at a desk somewhere,

looking at pictures of his family,

and maybe he has a secretary.

Maybe . . . he will be home in time for dinner.
We eat crackers and cheese and grapes, and drink
fizzy cranberry sodas from old-fashioned-looking
bottles
all before
Quinn's sister, who does not yell at us for wearing her
party dresses and her shoes,
comes home.
She does not have a gloomy face or a pierced tongue
either.
She does not grunt at us and close her door.
She smiles and asks Quinn about her day
and winks at me when she says she likes my name
and my hair
and my freckles.
The doorbell rings after a while and we are
still laughing about dancing and school
and the bump in my hair on picture day
when my dad walks in.
Let's go, kiddo, he says.
And I straighten up right away.
It would have been nice to have Quinn Mitchell meet
dog Mitchell,

but I'm glad it worked out this way.
I'd move in there in a heartbeat,
comma,
if I could bring James and Mom and Mitchell with me.
Period. End of sentence.

Field Trip

Outside Quinn's house is a brand-new sports car,
with James scrunched into the backseat.
Check it, he says,
rolling down the window.
I feel my face get hot because the car is so cool and
my brother is smiling
and the air isn't as frozen all of a sudden.
What's happening? I say, confused because it
isn't a dad night.
Wanted to take you all for a spin, Dad says,
hopping behind the steering wheel.
He drives James and me home—
shifting gears hard and fast, the way he does
even when he isn't driving—
to Mom's house, where she is already in pajamas,

cooking something—tacos—
in the kitchen.
Put on a coat, Dad says to her.
What? No, she says.
Mom, James says. *Put on a coat.*
Dad has already gone to the closet. He's carrying a
big black fur coat he must have dug up from the way
back.
I glance at James.
He sometimes goes through Mom's pockets for
change and I bet he missed this one,
and it looks fancy, like it might have more than just
loose change jangling around inside.
Are you crazy? Mom says.
But she puts it on and they leave us and we watch
from the window as the top on the car comes down,
turning somehow into a chariot.
It's like Cinderella, I say out loud.
Yeah, right, James says, and we just sit there, waiting.
They are gone so long we put our own tacos together.
I make a platter, the way Mom does,
lettuce in one pile, tomatoes in another, shredded
cheese and avocado slices.

Maybe he'll stay, I say. *Maybe it'll be taco night.*
Maybe you've read too many fairy tales, James says.
I think of Princess Atalanta.
I did really want her to settle down with Young John.
James is right.
The door slams, and a whoosh of cold air comes in
with Mom,
who throws that giant coat that used to be an animal
on the bench in the front hall.
Taco night! she says in a high voice that is her acting
voice, and she's not
the world's best actress.
I look over her shoulder at James,
who is taking great care to hang up the coat
and who pulls out a twenty-dollar bill from the
pocket.
A fairy tale for him.
Something else for Mom and me.
Beautiful platter, honey, she says.
I tried, I say.
Bibbidi-bobbidi-boo.

One Hundred Days

On the 100th day of school,
the teachers and the principal
and the specials teachers
and pretty much everyone who walks by you in the
hallway says *you are one hundred days smarter.*
So we are supposed to bounce a beach ball
100 times in the air
and count out 100 Cheerios and string them
on a necklace
and take
100 steps down the hall,
which Quinn and I choose to do together because
every time Quinn and I team up for something, we
end up having a better time than when we are paired
up with someone else.

We end up laughing mainly because she says things like
I'm going to count how many times my sister mutes her phone
while she's on with her boyfriend just so she can fart.
I bet it is one hundred.
Ewww, I say, and we laugh so hard I get the hiccups,
and then we count those too.
We never get to 100 because we are supposed to settle
down and write a list of new things we have learned
since the first day of school.
How are you 100 days smarter?
the paper says
at the top.
I stare at the paper and think about all that math,
the multiplication facts, the long division, and
all the books I have read and
all the pages I have logged in my reading log,
and I know I've done a lot of work in 100 days,
but it doesn't make me feel smarter,
just maybe tired
of answering questions.
I'm better at choosing friends, I write.

Social Studies

There is a group of people,
a tribe.
They never look each other in the eyes.
They stare and smile and laugh
out loud
at their hands,
which glow and reflect blue light on their faces.
And they throw things at each other,
still not looking,
flipping their hair,
picking at themselves,
at each other.
The females especially do this.
And some look sadder than they should be,
since the things they are throwing

are snowballs,
flung with gusto
into the air
at each other.
Warlike.
Flinging *themselves*
with gusto down the hill,
on sleds and flying saucers.
They can fly,
this tribe
of teenagers.
James woke me up by throwing snow pants
on my head.
Snow day!
And Mom made hot chocolate for breakfast
and eggs and toast when we usually have cereal
or a granola bar.
We watched giant flakes hit the windows
and the ground in piles
while Mom got ready for work.
Later, James dragged me out for sledding with
his friends,
the tribe that laughs at their hands,

two blocks from our house.
I think of the Iroquois league—the Cayuga, the
Onondaga, the Mohawk, the Seneca, the Oneida,
once fighting,
warlike.
Until they found peace.
Like me,
whizzing down the hill,
flying toward the teenage nation,
who are looking for something in the palms of their
glowing hands,
a glimpse
or a glimmer
of hope,
but not peace.

Assembly

They spend A LOT of time at school assemblies
telling you not to be a bully.
Sometimes they even start on the very first day,
when I can't even remember which classroom is mine
let alone how to be an *upstander,*
a word they invented for a person who stands up for
others when others are being bullied.
Another way of saying, a LOT to ask.
This year, they've waited until now,
until Valentine's Day,
to spread the love.
The name of the assembly is Spread the Love.
The principal reads us a book by that name,
and then one of the second-grade teachers I never

had comes in playing his guitar and singing really
loud—
"SPREAD THE LOVE," the song.
And all the other teachers start singing too,
and the whole school is clapping and singing along.
Quinn and I just look at each other in a funny way
because the whole thing is kind of weird.
Love is a funny thing to spread around an elementary
school.
Germs is more like it.
There's been a stomach virus going around and they
keep sending notices home and Mom
keeps calling us to ask if we've washed our hands.
Viruses are easy to spread around but love is not.
Just ask Jackson "FINGER SLAMMER"
Allen. He is a spreader of misery, and Quinn and I
spend a lot of time avoiding him and his group of
FOUR ANNOYING BOYS,
germs, all of them.
So we're supposed to go back to our classrooms and
make valentines for each other, which means I have to
make one for Jackson.

I want to write *what does it feel like to have two names*
that could be last names or first names?
I want to write *does it feel the same as getting your finger*
slammed in between a chair and a table?
But I just write *Happy Valentine's Day!*
Because of the bullying assembly.
Afterward, at indoor recess, I look over at
Lilly with two *l*'s.
She is reading a book and even though she doesn't
look sad or anything, I get up and go over to her.
Want to join our no-friend club? I say.
Sure, she says. She doesn't seem to care
what the no-friend club is,
or maybe she loves the play like I do.
She and Quinn and I are working on our valentines
and I say *Lilly, do you still have those toys you were*
holding on to for that princess superhero from Mars?
Huh? she says.
Then she starts coloring again.
Then she says *do you still eat your shirts?*
Huh? I say, because I don't really want Quinn to know
that I ate through a lot of my clothes in kindergarten.

Nerves, Mom would say.
Disgusting, Dad would say.
But I get what she's saying, so I laugh
and then I put my shirt in my mouth
and get back to coloring.

Line Leader,
Part One

When you are part of a group and that group is made
up of FOUR ANNOYING BOYS,
you yourself are probably annoying.
It is possible, Mom says, that you are NOT annoying,
that at home you are sweet and funny
and nice to your little sister,
but Mom doesn't know you like I do.
I protect you from her and you don't even know it.
I tell her things like *he would have told on me for*
kicking him when I was just walking normally and his
leg got CAUGHT on my leg by ACCIDENT.
And she says things like *but he didn't*
and
oh, he probably just likes you a lot.
I say

ick.

And also

not true.

Not even close.

You liking me is worse than you hating me.

Mom, for once in her life, is wrong.

I have been protecting you long enough.

Because today—

TODAY—

I was busy being a nice person and checking on Ezra

when he was crying in the hallway

and we were lined up,

quiet and single file.

Thinking back, he was probably crying because of

something you and your

ANNOYING friends did to him.

He told me to get lost,

which was also ANNOYING, because I didn't even

really want to check on him,

except I heard Mom's voice in my head

telling me to reach out when someone needs

reaching out to.

But you.

YOU looked right at me and said something worse
than the ONE MILLION TIMES you have called
me MEDUSA so far this year.
Worse than the ONE MILLION TIMES you have
pretended to turn to stone
when you look at my face.
Is Ezra crying because you're so ugly? you asked,
fake-pouting.
I thought about hitting you.
I even made a fist.
The only thing that stopped me was the idea that
I would definitely get in trouble, and I HATE
getting in trouble
more than I hate you.
Or maybe it's a tie.
(And not a happily-ever-after,
Princess-Atalanta-and-Young-John-running-in-a-race-
in-a-fairy-tale kind of a tie.)
Mom was not happy with you.
She ALMOST called your mom.
Almost.
(to be continued)

Art

We have spent a lot of time making color wheels.
I love mine so much
I protect it between two sheets of regular paper and
roll it up and put a rubber band
around the tube I made.
At Dad's house I take it upstairs and
lay it out on the floor to admire it.
I wanted to wait until I was home
with Mom.
She would love it.
She would like that I was so careful
about staying in the lines.
That I took extra time with a very fine black Sharpie
to fill in my own copyright line, as if

I were an art company that specializes in making
color wheels for fourth graders
to help them learn about primary and
complementary colors.
She would love that.
I have a friend who would like that, my dad says from
the doorway,
startling me.
He has two paperweights in his hand—
one is a heavy glass circle
that says *University of Pennsylvania*
in etched white letters.
The other is a heavy and smooth black stone from
I don't know where.
He bends down and puts one on each side of the
color wheel,
which fights to roll back up again.
Her name is Stephanie.
She's an art teacher, he says.
An artist.
Okay, I say.
I stare at the warm side of the wheel
because my art teacher,

whose name is definitely NOT Stephanie,

taught us that some colors have to do with our moods.

The warm ones are for happiness. The cool ones, for
sadness.

Pessimism, she said.

I try not to look at the cool blues

because I am an optimist, Mom says.

Always looking at the bright side.

Line Leader, Part Two

There are some things Mom doesn't need to know.
There are some things that can be a secret forever
because they are special to two people and only two
people.
I stopped Mom from calling your mom for a reason.
The reason is Quinn.
I didn't even know that Quinn had seen
what happened,
but she must have, even though she was at the way front,
the line leader.
Well, Quinn bent over,
and no one knew why but the line moved along
without her,
without its leader,
until,

somehow,
YOU tripped over the foot she must have only stuck
out because she was tying her shoelace
(and not because she wanted to trip you).
Well, you flew
across the hall and smack into Ezra,
who must have ALSO had enough of you
because he made a fist.
And well,
hating you and hating getting in trouble are
apparently
not a tie for him
since you ended up bent over too,
and not because your shoelace was untied.
And maybe I even saw a tear.
Quinn's eyes lit up and mine might have too,
which is terrible,
and I'm sorry.
And that is why I didn't let my mom call your mom.
It's all right to cry.
We are even.

Principal's Office

When I grow up I do not want to be in charge of a
whole bunch of kids who do not listen
unless the principal is the one talking.
Even if they make funny faces
behind the principal's back,
everyone listens when she talks,
everyone listens when she says *boys and girls* in a way
that sounds nice when you're in kindergarten and first
grade but that, by fourth grade,
starts to sound a little annoying.
When I was in second grade I won a bookmark design
contest—
Reading takes you places,
I wrote
on the side of a rocket

on its way to the moon.

Well, I got to make the morning announcements as
my prize.

I was nervous so I stared at a sign—

The princiPAL is your PAL!

to distract myself.

I think I didn't know then,

in second grade,

that there was another way to spell *principal*.

That a principle was something else entirely,

something that might also take you places.

I think now that the sign isn't about spelling at all.

I think maybe our principal thinks this sign

makes her seem friendly.

Like calling us *boys and girls* with a wide grin

and clenched teeth.

Two whole years later, I stare at the sign while I wait

to read from *Free to Be . . . You and Me*

over the loudspeaker

and to distract myself from Jackson Allen's sweat.

He is standing too close to me and we just had gym

and he won a million races and

his sweat is contagious.

My clothes feel itchy.

Free to Be . . . You and Me is part of the whole school's
theme this year,

not just the fourth grade.

Not just the fourth class.

Other grades aren't doing a play

but a collage,

or a video,

or a poetry collection

of things they learned from *Free to Be . . . You and Me.*

It is a school-wide endeavor.

There is a bulletin board outside the main office to
prove it.

Almost every last fourth grader has gotten a chance to
read from our show

over the loudspeaker.

Once a week the teachers choose another group to go.

This time it is Jackson Allen,

three other ANNOYING BOYS,

and me.

I stare at the PrinciPAL sign and ignore the
sweating boys.

We each take a line and then we read—

read, not sing—our part.
I am last.
I say
I might be pretty;
you might grow tall.
And all together,
in unison,
we say
but we don't have to change at all.
I have just said,
in front of everyone,
I might be pretty.
My head fills up with pressure.
Like his sweat, Jackson's hot red cheeks are contagious,
spreading to mine.
He snorts.
This is my punishment, I think,
for feeling happy when he got hit
by Ezra
in line
the other day.
I have been sent to the principal's office,
on principle.

Spring Break

Where are you off to?
Have you been to Saint Maarten?
No? It's gorgeous this time of year.
Just what the doctor ordered!
We all need a break, right?
Not the kids—us!
This is how the parents talk at the supermarket
while I decide which gum to chew on our trip to
Florida—
Juicy Fruit!—
while Mom smiles and asks questions about places we
will never go,
because when she takes a vacation, she wants to be
with her mom,

with sunglasses
with a *good book on a beach,*
where she can
just be.
I love it too, starting
with the music that plays when the baggage claim
starts up and spits out bags, one at a time—
tropical music that welcomes you to a place so friendly
the warm air hugs you
when you walk out into the night.
Welcome to Fort Lauderdale.
We spend time at the beach,
at Nana's pool,
reading good books,
being
with each other and by ourselves
while James spends time with his music,
sharing it with us only when the volume is turned up
so loud his headphones vibrate
with the extra sound.
I don't think he heard the tropical music at the
baggage claim or the quiet

in the car rental garage at the airport,
or the waves or the kids—
over there!
They must be five or so
making a tunnel that will collapse into itself later on
at high tide.
I sit with my legs straight and try to bury them
myself.
No luck.
I throw a flip-flop at James, and he startles and gives
me a *what the*—*?* look.
BURY ME, I mouth.
He ignores me, closing both eyes and then opening
one back up.
I pout.
He throws off his headphones and his bad attitude
and gets burying.
I win! I am five years old again and he is ten.
Now it's the sand that's hugging me,
and my brother,
and the waves break,
and the sand

laid thick on top of me
breaks,
freeing me,
like this break from the end of winter,
the beginning of
spring.

Colonial Fair

The minute we get back, we have to finish up our
Colonial Fair projects.
I made a diorama from one of James's giant
shoe boxes.
It is a colonial classroom.
Mom and I went through my dollhouse for wooden
things, got chalkboard paper at a craft store, made a
classroom that made me think of
Little House on the Prairie.
We brought in our dioramas yesterday and we
oohed and aahed at each other's handiwork.
Some of the boys used Legos, and I felt jealous of their
modern little boxes.
Today, at the Colonial Fair, we will stand by our
dioramas,

dressed in character,
and present our reports to the other grades.
I will be a teacher—
a colonial teacher.
It's easier to think about what you might have been
than what you'll be.
I need a bonnet!
I say to my dad in the morning.
I forgot about the bonnet, I say,
careful not to seem upset.
I have my dress and my apron, I say.
I want to cry but don't want him to be mad that these
things only happen
at his house
on his night.
Dad goes into a closet in his apartment,
his apartment that echoes when you take steps on the
hardwood floors,
echoes when you make a phone call late at night
to your mom.
He pulls out a snow hat with flaps for the ears.
No thanks, I say, scrunching up my nose.
It snowed a lot then, he says. *The winters were hard.*

I think this is more interesting than a bonnet, he says.
Be the girl in the snow hat, he says.
Let the other girls be the ones in the bonnets.
I carry the hat in my lap in the backseat of the
sports car.
I carry it in my hand,
behind my back,
when I walk into the classroom.
I watch all the other girls put on their bonnets.
Did you forget yours, Isabel? Mrs. Soto asks.
I've got plenty of extras, she says.
Mrs. Soto is very excited about the Colonial Fair.
I think she would have been a teacher back then too.
No, I say. *I've got a snow hat,*
with earflaps.
The winters were hard, I say.
Even better than a bonnet, she says.
Kids from other classrooms come to each station,
and I tell them all about my colonial classroom.
I wear my hat the whole time
and Quinn stands next to me in her bonnet,
barely talking.

She's a nurse, so I think maybe she's being quiet so her diorama patients can rest.

She says she's cold.

I've got a snow hat, I say.

Trade ya! I say.

She can be the girl in the snow hat now.

I'll be the one in the bonnet.

Nurse

I am hyperventilating.
I cannot breathe.
I cannot talk.
I ran so fast I wished the gym teacher could have seen.
She should have given me a reason to run
in the first place,
and I would have passed those phys ed tests
with flying colors.
Today I would pass.
Today I would be the best.
Help!
Running and yelling even after the teachers came,
even after the nurse came,
even after the ambulance came.
All because,

before she was in the fourth class,
before she ever lived here,
Quinn was in
and out
of a hospital
for a year.
I am still out of breath.
But I do not have asthma.
Neither does Quinn.
It is something else.
Cancer.
Or it was.
Before she was my new favorite person,
she spent most of her time throwing up the horrible
medicine that is supposed to kill the cancer but it kills
everything else too, everything in sight.
Even the good stuff.
Even the stuff that helps you through cold season,
says the poster in the pediatrician's office, warning
nervous parents not to ask for antibiotics.
Obviously, my dad muttered
at that poster,
annoyed at it or at me

the only time he ever took me there without Mom,
his doctor-ness showing up also for the first time.
He hides it otherwise, pretending he is something else,
in some other business where no one asks you for
advice.
She'll have some tests, Quinn's parents are saying now
to the nurse,
who is worried sick.
I am dizzy still.
I tried to catch her, but she fell in a heap
off the thing that spins so fast
I've seen more than one person actually throw up
from it.
The moms worry about the spinning and maybe
someone getting hurt.
I only worry about the throwing up.
Until now.
Until I saw Quinn Mitchell, bossy and smart and
excellent at building and planning and being a
president,
fall in that heap, eyes rolled back.
She's going to be okay, her mother said to me.
She's run-down.

We've been through this before.
If we have to do it again,
we will.
I wish I could call my dad,
but he'd stay quiet, probably
pretending not to be a doctor.
Are you okay, honey? Quinn's dad asks me as they
wheel Quinn away
on a stretcher.
She is awake and she smiles at me.
I smile back.
Yes, I say.
I am pretending too.

Reading Log

I don't tell anyone at home what happened,
don't tell them I was there,
that I heard all about the cancer
that they pretended was something else.
Something with a long name and an abbreviation that
is supposed to make me think it isn't terrible.
I go about my business, as they say.
I do my nightly reading log.
Stargirl keeps me company.
I had thought it was over between *Stargirl* and me
until Quinn told me there was a sequel.
And now we're together again and I partly want to
read it fast and I partly want to read it slow, since all
that's left after this is the *Stargirl* journal,

which is just a place to write,
and all you really need for that is your head
and a piece of paper.
But I will get the journal for Quinn for her birthday,
or maybe
for a get-well-soon present, because we love *Stargirl*.
We.
Quinn and I.
Quinn and me.
Are we best friends? We never discussed it,
never had a real no-friend club meeting.
I don't even know when her birthday is.
I will get her the journal anyway, and I will write a
note on the inside,
the way my grandmother does when she buys me
a book.
With so much love,
Grammy.
Mine will say:
To the great Quinn Mitchell, president of the no-friend
club, in charge of everything,
Love, Izzy Kline, vice president, in charge of entertainment.

I would like to write *best friends forever* also, but I'll decide about that later.

I practice it in the margins of my reading log.

Love, Stargirl

45 minutes

pages 91–128

best friends forever.

Music

There is another person in the fourth grade who can sing and it is not Quinn, since Quinn isn't even here to audition.

It is Lilly with two *l*'s.

Turns out Lilly loves the play as much as I do because she gets the best part,

the part I kind of wanted.

Kind of with all my heart.

There are a couple of solos in the show, and I got a teeny one, a small part of a small song called "Glad to Have a Friend Like You."

But I am not glad.

I want the one Lilly with two *l*'s got and the whole way home I think

Oh, everyone just LOVES LILLY, all of a sudden.

LOVES LILLY'S PERFECT VOICE.
LOVES THE WAY SHE SINGS WITH FEELING.
I'm shouting these things in my head all the way home,
shouting so, so loud in my head.
And I am so, so MAD,
I run into the bathroom and I throw up.
I thought I maybe made myself sick
with all that head shouting.
But I did not.
Unless jealousy can also cause a fever.

Sick Day

Because I threw up, Mom is nervous.
She even calls my dad to see if maybe,
possibly,
he could stay with me.
But that would mean rescheduling patients, he tells her.
But the smell—she says.
I'm not sure I can handle—she says.
I am a patient to my mom, who is impatient herself
with Dad
and his hanging up quickly.
I can tell by the way she holds the phone to her ear
even after he is gone.
But the throwing-up part is over anyway, and now it
is the soup-and-TV part,
the part Mom is really good at,

the part where she puts on old shows on the classic
channel and we watch them all,
and she talks about her days off from school as a kid
and we play hangman
and color old coloring books
and she introduces me to *Bewitched,*
a show where the mom is a witch who can do
all kinds of things just by wiggling her nose and it's
kind of a terrible show but it makes her smile
so we watch a marathon and color.
Ding, dong.
Mom and I look at each other because no one ever
rings a doorbell unless they have been invited or food
has been ordered.
I feel a little better, I say, getting up but not really
wanting to get up out of our cozy corner of the sofa,
not really wanting to feel all better,
just a little better, because it would be so nice to have
one more day like this.
Old shows and Lipton soup and laughs that make
those sore throw-up muscles hurt,
and flowers.
The doorbell is a flower delivery.

Something that doesn't smell like throw-up.
Love,
Dad.
It's easy to forget because he is so organized and
serious and because he loves art and classical music
and also jazz, which drives my mom crazy,
that he is also funny.
Flowers from Dad, I say.
He's good at flowers, my mom says.
I put the flowers on the table. Our flowers.
I plop back down into my spot but have to get up
again, almost immediately.
The flowers are blocking the view of *Bewitched.*
The flowers that should really be for someone who
needs them.
If only I could just wiggle my nose, I think.

A Note from the PTA

As you may have heard, fourth grader Quinn Mitchell was taken to the hospital by ambulance this week after falling ill on the playground, it says.

The Mitchell family has asked us to communicate on their behalf. Quinn is a fighter, it says.

She has battled and won the fight against acute lymphoblastic leukemia once before, and if that is the diagnosis,

if this is a relapse,

we are certain she will win again, it says.

In the meantime, we at the PTA encourage you to communicate with your children about their feelings and concerns. We also encourage you to please keep the Mitchell family in your thoughts while they investigate the cause of Quinn's current condition.

Mom looks at the paper and looks back at me.

Oh, honey, she says.

I'm fine, I say, taking the paper back from her.

The paper she found in my folder, and which she was looking for because another mom had already called about it.

She's fine, I say, tucking the paper back into the pocket of my folder,

the folder I picked to be my take-home folder for the new school year.

The one with puppies on it

that was going to cheer me up each day about having the yelling teacher and

Lilly with two *l*'s and no one else.

It's going to be fine, I say.

I think we should talk about it, Mom says.

I think I have a lot of homework, I say.

I give her a big, wide smile and I nod a big, slow nod to let her know

I have not lost my sense of humor.

It

is

going

to

be

okay,

I say slowly

and loudly.

As if she doesn't speak English.

As if I know it for a fact.

As if I am a grown-up,

a member of the PTA,

writing letters home about things I know nothing about.

Rehearsal

Lilly and I stand side by side today,
the day after my sick day
the day after
the day after
she got the part I wanted.
The day after my mom found out that Quinn had
collapsed.
When Lilly belts out
"When We Grow Up," I understand completely
why she got that part and
I don't feel sick about it anymore.
I will be part of the chorus.
I will say my "Glad to Have a Friend Like You" lines
with gusto,

because I'm glad not to be throwing up anymore,
glad to have a part,
glad for my friends in the no-friend club,
and our president,
in charge of everything,
who I will gladly stand next to at the show,
which is turning out to be more of a concert
anyway—
with us standing
in rows
on the steps
of the stage.
Little groups of us will take a place on the stage
in the spotlight
for the acting parts or for the solo parts.
Lilly and I whisper to each other as we practice,
as others practice—
Fiona and Sara and the Candy Land party girls dancing,
a group of girls doing a skit to "Girl Land."
The whole group clapping through "Sisters and Brothers."
The funny kid who speaks the
"Don't Dress Your Cat in an Apron" part

and he himself will wear an apron and we might even
get a real, live cat in an apron on the stage,
and won't that be funny, if a cat is in an apron,
standing in a row with us,
Mrs. Johnson says.
We laugh and gasp at this.
But oh! When Jackson Allen sings *mommies are people*
we are silent.
Jackson Allen saying *mommy*
is all I can think about.
A bully saying *mommy* is as funny as a cat in an apron
except not in a ha-ha way
but in a silent way.
Jackson Allen *singing* the *mommies are people* part of
the "Parents Are People" song
(and he sings it well)
is all I can think about
until he throws down his sheet of paper with the
words on it and Mrs. Johnson says
Stick with it, buddy.
Turns the whole thing on its head if a young man sings
this part.

Young man.

Ha.

Between the real, live cat and this,

I've never been more glad to have a music teacher like

Mrs. Johnson.

Mrs. Johnson is a genius.

Camp Friends

Mom makes us eat dinner together because of the
news about Quinn.

She brings me home a big bag of Jelly Bellys, which
are just about my favorite thing in the world, and I see
that the bag is heavy on the watermelon oncs.

Thank you, I say in a whisper.

I want to yell *thank you* out loud at the top of my
lungs, but that would be like celebrating and

I am afraid to celebrate something like an abundance of
watermelon Jelly Bellys when Quinn is in the hospital.

I decide I will collect all of the watermelon Jelly Bellys
and save them until she is better,

until we can eat them together.

But then James brings up summer camp,

and the same way I am afraid of school projects,

I am afraid of sleepaway camp,
of meeting friends who you only get to have
for a few weeks.
The one exciting thing about it is the possibility that
I might meet my twin,
like in *The Parent Trap*,
and then we could switch lives for a while.
But now I watch James leaning his chair backward,
teetering the way he does,
and he gets a mean look.
Didn't I have a friend
at that awful camp?
he starts to say.
And I know what he's talking about and
I want him to stop.
James, my mom says, shaking her head
in my direction.
Yeah, I did, he says anyway.
And he was fine all summer and then we started getting
those letters from his mom.
James, my mom says again.
Stop it, I say now, into my spaghetti and meatballs.

My hand is holding on tight to the bag of jelly beans,
like it's a stress squeezie ball.
Stop what? he says.
Mom, what was his name?
STOP IT! I yell now, the way I've wanted to yell
all week.
The way I've wanted to yell since two years ago,
or maybe since forever.
STOP!
The one who died, he says anyway,
of cancer.
I scream and I throw the bag as hard as I can
at the wall,
and there are jelly beans everywhere but I don't
stay to watch,
to see where they settle.
This is not the same, Izzy, my mom calls after me.
It is not the same.
I go to my room and I feel sad
and sorry.
Sad that James's camp friend,
whose name was William,

whose name I will never forget,
died.
I remember the letters and the picture of him with
no hair.
I remember that my mom cried when she got the
final letter and that she was worried about how James
would feel.
I remember that James shrugged and walked away.
I feel sad about that.
And sorry about a million other things,
but mostly because I threw the Jelly Bellys.
I'm really sorry I won't have the watermelon Jelly Bellys
to give Quinn
when she's all better.

Guidance Counseling

I have never been mad at James before now,
not even when I should have been.
Like when we were much younger and playing airplane
and I was balancing him on my feet.
I was supporting him all by myself.
It was exciting.
He was flying.
Until he wasn't.
I let go, I guess.
Wasn't as strong as I thought,
I guess.
And his knee landed in the middle of my stomach.
In the spot that makes you stop breathing.
I still remember what it felt like,
that sucking feeling and how scary it was.

And I remember that my dad walked in right then,
unfortunately.
I wasn't mad at James,
but he was.
Or maybe he was mad at something else,
like my mom says,
and not at us.
And the mad mostly simmers, she says,
like the meat on the stove
on taco night.
But sometimes
it boils,
and sometimes it burns.
He picked up James,
boiling over,
I think.
You want to know how that feels?
But I didn't want James to know how it felt.
I was okay with him not knowing.
And Dad swung him—
ALMOST SWUNG HIM—
across the arm of the sofa.

I breathed finally when he put James back down
and I was still the only one in the room
who knew how it felt.
We were back to a simmer.
That is why it wasn't so bad that Dad moved out.
Why we could all breathe easier
once he was gone.
But it was important to me
to tell the counselor
that I was not mad at Dad,
not really mad at James,
not upset with Mom.
I was okay.
I just wanted everyone else
to be okay too.
But we're here because of Quinn, he says—
this counselor, who Mom thought I should talk to,
who works for the school, and who is
free and available,
and a great resource.
Because your mom is worried that you are worried, he says.
Mom is worried because you've lost a lot, he says.

I'm not worried, I say, but he is looking at me hard,
the way grown-ups do when they want proof.
I haven't lost anything, I say.
The divorce is a loss, he explains.
The divorce is a change, I say, *not a loss.*
He smiles
the way grown-ups do when you say something that
makes sense.
Even if it's a relapse, I say,
we'll get through it.
I like Quinn's mom so much I copy her.
That's all the guidance I need.

Science

In the name of science
we are investigating the way things change.
My teacher says change is caused by a catalyst.
Jackson "FINGER SLAMMER" Allen is my partner.
Into the test tube, Jackson pours more of the stuff that
makes things fizz,
and a little more,
too much of it.
I eye the teacher
because I am a rule follower and Jackson is not and
she is not looking so I don't stop him from pouring in
a little more
and we watch it bubble up
before our eyes.
I'm afraid to touch it but I do.

I scoot my test tube in the direction of Jackson.
In the name of science.
And there it goes!
Up and up until a little poof.
A spitting, oozing poof of stuff,
matter,
all over Jackson's face.
I snort.
I laugh so hard
I fall off my chair.
I get back up and try to record my findings.
Next to catalyst, I write
Jackson.

Rounds

Miss Hall who is now Mrs. Johnson
wants us to sing in rounds.
It is her way of making the show her own.
Our own.
It sounds pretty,
the circular way we are singing,
looping in and out of each other's place in the song
until we sing again
all at once.
Looping the way my dad does
all around the hospital
when he makes his rounds,
visiting the patients who do not know that he has ever
had a temper at all.
That he grits his teeth sometimes in a way that

makes me feel

not afraid

but sad

that he is mad.

But now,

and maybe because he is away from us

and closer to Stephanie,

he is more like he is with his patients.

Patient.

This is the place in the round

where I want to say that Dad,

just because he has a temper,

just because he has lost his temper

once or maybe twice

in the past,

is coming around

more and more.

Even called me today to say that he stopped in

to see Quinn,

that he chatted with her mom,

that she was doing great,

that it probably wasn't a relapse,

that she has the flu,

that she will be okay.
And then
he asks if I'm okay.
Me.
I smile into the phone and say *uh-huh*.
This is the part
where he admits he is a doctor
and a father
all at once.

Geometry

One of the FOUR ANNOYING BOYS put a note in
my backpack
and it had to be unfolded and
unfolded and
unfolded,
otherwise it would have just stayed a tiny little triangle
forever.
Instead it was this:
Isabel makes me
Scared to look
At her
Because she mite turn me to stone
Even though she is sometimes funny and smart and a
Little bit pretty
An acrostic.

It seems like this could be written by the
FINGER-SLAMMING,
MEDUSA-CALLING
Jackson Allen.
Someone wanted me to believe that he wrote it.
Someone who follows after Jackson
like he is the PRESIDENT OF THE
FOUR ANNOYING BOYS CLUB
or something.
But Jackson Allen did not write this poem.
If someone wanted me to believe that,
they would have to do a better job.
Jackson Allen, who I have known since kindergarten,
who my mom used to call cute because of his dimples,
has always been, ever since kindergarten,
the best speller in the class, which I know for a FACT
because I am always the second-best speller.
And when you are the second-best at something,
you always know who is the first-best.
So this note, unfolded into the shape of a rectangle,
was written by someone else
who is not even in the top ten spellers.
Mite?

He should have to write it 100 times on
the whiteboard.
Might might might might might might might . . .
Until he learns that if you are pretending to be
someone else, you MIGHT want to
shape up in the pretending department.
I saw on TV that when a person says something nice
to you,
you should accept.
You should say
Why, thank you.
You should do this so you appear confident
even if you are not.
Even if you don't think you are funny or smart
or a little bit pretty.
But she didn't say what to do if the compliment comes
in the shape
of something else.

Phys Ed

I step on the scale and back up.
When she puts the metal stick on my head I look
sideways at my mom,
who is clapping her hands
for my achievement.
Two whole inches and one quarter inch since last year.
Niiiice, Mom says. *Way to grow. Get it? Grow?*
I get it.
I try not to laugh at her because she can be so
EMBARRASSING with her clapping and
snorting when things are funny to her
and only to her.
I laugh anyway.
The doctor takes the cold stethoscope to my back first

and then to my chest.

I laugh at the cold.

Laugh again when she pushes on my belly,

takes a peek under my gown,

to see what's what.

To see if anything is *doing* yet.

Mom's smile is bright and hopeful,

like she's wishing for something,

but I don't know what.

The same way I don't know what I am wishing for.

Don't know if I am for the *what's what*

or against it.

Lilly with two *l*'s has two of something else

too.

I try not to look,

try not to straighten out her shirt where it bunches

around her bra.

A real bra,

not a tight half tank top,

like I wear some days

when my shirt is too loose,

making me feel too loose

underneath.

You are exactly where you should be, kiddo,
the doctor says.
Not too fast,
not too slow.
Just right.
My mom gives me a big squeeze before we get in the car.
Great checkup, baby! she says.
And I realize
we were wishing
for the same thing.

Rules

We watch some more of the *Free to Be . . . You and Me*
video at the end of school today. There are still some
parts we haven't seen.
We're working on the "Sisters and Brothers" song for
the show, so Mrs. Soto thought we might like to see
the part where Marlo Thomas interviews all these
1970s-looking kids about their sisters
and brothers.
They say funny things about their brothers hitting
them in the face,
which isn't so funny in real life but seems funny in
this video.
Reminds me of playing the card game
bloody knuckles with James when I was much younger

and so was he.
The loser of the game gets their knuckles rapped with
the whole deck of cards and it is supposed to hurt,
if you're playing for real.
It's a rule.
We're no pretenders, James and I.
We are card game rule followers.
James made it hurt when I lost,
and I made it hurt back when he lost.
And it was a by-the-rules game of bloody knuckles.
No pretending.
We were so proud of ourselves,
even if Mom was not proud of us
at all.
We mopped up our knuckles with wet paper towels and
watched the blood spread into the watery paper and we
creeped each other out for a long while,
laughing and annoying Mom.
Something tells me Marlo Thomas would not approve
either.
She keeps asking these kids
over and over

if they like their sisters and brothers and they all keep
saying no
and laughing.
We're not supposed to like them is what I think when
I watch this.
Or we're not supposed to say we do.
It's a rule.
After the interview, a whole big group of grown-ups
get together and sing and clap about brothers and
sisters and
ain't we lucky, which just sounds so funny because
who says *ain't?*
When we pack up our things to leave for the day
I ask Lilly
if she likes her brother or sister
and she says she doesn't have one
and that she wished she did.
Brother or sister? I ask.
A big brother, she says.
They know everything and
they take care of bullies for you, she says.
I think of something the little kid in the interview
says about his brother

near the end.

Sometimes you're good to me and sometimes you're bad,
but I love you.

Something no one would ever say in real life,
if you're playing by the rules.

Time-Out

I walk by James's room and the door is closed and we
haven't done very much talking to each other since he
brought up William,
since he couldn't even remember William's name.
He spends most of his time with the other teenagers
anyway,
or behind his locked door
with headphones on.
Usually I slow down in front of his room and maybe
I hope he'll open up,
unlock, and let me in.
Usually, but not today.
I hurry by, to my room.
Hey, he says, standing at my door,

where he usually never stands unless I beg him to wait
until I am ready,
for him to turn off my light for me
at bedtime,
his finger on the light switch plate from my grandmother
from Pennsylvania,
which has a little girl on it, getting a boost from her
brother,
reaching up to *outen the light,* it says.
Something they maybe say, or said
a long time ago,
in Pennsylvania.
I have something for you, he says, scraping his teeth
against the ring
in his tongue.
That's gross, I say.
He shrugs and I follow him to his room,
where he throws a bag of something at me.
I catch it because I am good at catching things
in a hurry.
Jelly Bellys.
Mom made me clean them up, he says.

Kitchen-floor Jelly Bellys? I say.

Take 'em or leave 'em, he says.

I take 'em.

Then he hands me headphones and

he puts on headphones too, and we lie down on the floor, head to head

and he plays me some music.

Real music, he says.

The Beatles! he shouts over the loud, weird sounds of someone—

John Lennon! he shouts—

singing:

I am the eggman.

They are the eggmen.

I am the walrus.

It's a magical mystery tour, I think.

James is my guide, I think.

Sometimes he kicks me out and sometimes

he takes me along for the ride.

Early Dismissal

Quinn is home,
dismissed early from the hospital,
with a diagnosis that requires a regular old letter home
from the nurse.
Like lice,
or strep throat.
Your child might have been exposed to the flu virus.
A student was recently diagnosed with influenza.
A student.
Suddenly Quinn is anonymous.
It's better that way.
The PTA sent their own letter, with Quinn's full name,
explaining the wonderful outcome,
the relief we all feel,
knowing that it wasn't a recurrence,

knowing that her collapse was

due to extreme fatigue and fever,

that she is simply battling the flu.

My mom gives me a big, long hug after she reads

both notes.

The flu! she screams.

She does a funny little dance and we jump around the

kitchen, cheering and singing, and she's crying at the

same time.

You hardly even know her, I say.

But you do, she says.

And then she looks up at the ceiling,

and closes her eyes,

and says

There but for the grace of God.

You're weird, I say.

You are, she says, and hugs me again and tighter.

Overflow Table

Why didn't you tell me about the cancer? I ask
since it is our overflow day,
the day when Quinn and I get to sit together
at the table for all the kids
who don't fit
at the class lunch table.
There is a chart that tells us whose day it is, and
I dread it every time.
It is the worst day usually.
You never know who else will be there.
People from other classes too.
People you aren't used to anymore.
Sometimes it is Fiona,
sometimes Sara,
sometimes Jackson.

Today it is Quinn, so it doesn't matter who else is there.

(Okay, it matters.

Sara and Fiona are there.)

I forgot, I guess, Quinn says.

Do you even have asthma? I ask.

She shakes her head no and looks at her plate.

I thought you fell, I say,

that day.

Didn't I? Quinn asks.

I think you fainted, I say.

Was it cool? she asks, her eyes looking up at me and

not at the

Homemade Baked Ziti from the lunch menu.

Cool? Fiona asks.

Sara just stares. Sara has never liked things like this.

Scary things that not everyone thinks of as scary.

Scary things that can be funny if you choose funny

over scary,

like Quinn does.

Was it like this? Quinn says, and she throws herself off

the bench and onto the

disgusting cafeteria floor.

I squint and say

no, more like this,

and I clunk my head down on the table and stick my
tongue out.

Really? she squeals.

And we are laughing the way we laughed at her house
in our party dresses.

I snort, even.

Sara and Fiona are looking at us out of the corners of
their eyes,

pretending it isn't funny.

One day I will ask Quinn what it was like to have
cancer, since I am wondering

if she thought about dying,

if she threw up a lot,

if there was a lot of crying,

if she worries every day about it coming back,

if the flu feels even worse when the flu could be cancer.

One day I will ask her, when I am not
overflowing
with relief.

Lemonade Stand

It smells like spring, which means people are in the
mood for sweet drinks and cookies.
Or else maybe they are in the mood to lay out a towel
on the grass,
kick off their shoes,
like we did,
like Quinn and I did at recess.
The day started out cold and *if you come in with a coat,*
you go out with a coat.
A silly rule, if you ask me.
I mean, you don't go out to recess with your backpack
and you come in with *that* the same
way you come in with a coat.
But we bring our Windbreakers and we toss them in a
pile and we fly high on the swings,

kicking off our shoes and one of them, my right-foot
shoe, hits Fiona,
and she says
hey!
And I think of the flying piñata at Sara's Candy Land
birthday party and I just can't even
believe how we don't talk to each other so much
anymore.
How we used to swing together and talk together and
laugh together and dance together
and make lemonade stands together on days like this.
And it's all because of soccer and maybe dance and
being in the fourth class.
And I wonder if we were only friends because of being
near each other and not because
of being close to each other.
Quinn and I spread out our Windbreakers on the
grass and put our faces up to the sun.
Let's make a lemonade stand today, I say.
And we do, outside Quinn's big house right near
Main Street,
later in the afternoon.
And people walk past and a few buy lemonade.

But then Fiona and Sara walk by and Fiona says
Ralph's is opening today, most people want ices and not
lemonade.
And I say *well, Ralph's isn't giving their money to charity.*
And I point to my sign, which says
All proceeds go to Marlo Thomas's St. Jude's Hospital for
Sick Kids.
And they shrug and walk away.
And Quinn and I go on selling lemonade and cookies
to people on their way to Ralph's
opening day, who toss their filled-up cups in the
garbage can
about a block down the road.

Butterfly Problems

I don't notice until the day of the concert, when I see
in the program
Lilly Callahan, "When We Grow Up"
that Lilly with two *l*'s actually has four *l*'s in her name
(five if you count the first one)
and I think
that's a lot of *l*'s.
And then I find out that she is sick—regular sick—and
I feel bad about it, since I can only imagine how awful
it would be to miss out on singing a solo,
especially with a voice as nice as hers.
But then Mrs. Johnson asks me if I know the words
and I say I do.
And suddenly those butterflies, the ones from that
first night into day

before the first day of school,

they're back.

I fill up the minutes until the show starts with

will I be good enough?

Not *will Dad show up?*, which is what I thought I'd

be thinking about.

Not *will Mom remember?*, which I also thought I'd

be thinking a lot about.

Not *I hope James skips out of school for this*, which he

told me he might do and which I actually believe

because James hates school and because James doesn't

care about getting in trouble the way I do.

It's May, I think. *School is almost over*, I think.

The *Free to Be* project is almost over, too, which is

okay because I might finally be tired of these songs.

So Dad shows up and he's with his art teacher friend

and I think that I hate her because she wears a lot of

jewelry and perfume.

I can tell she has perfume even from all the way on

the stage.

She looks perfumed.

The principal introduces us right after she explains the

school-wide theme and that the fourth grade has done

a marvelous job and she can't wait to share it with
everyone.
It gets quiet.
Quinn gives my hand a squeeze and says *go!*
I head onto the stage, into the spotlight.
I start to sing Lilly's song and I don't sing it so well
until I spot Mom's face,
her plain, pretty face.
Then I get back to singing the way I sing.
With feeling.
The light is shining on the outside of me,
but it is on the inside
that I feel
lit up.
I never thought about the magic of butterflies until now.
I only ever thought about the trouble with butterflies.
The first-day butterflies.
The divorce butterflies.
The meeting-Dad's-art-teacher-girlfriend butterflies.
Butterfly problems,
all of them.
When I finish, people clap so loud I feel dizzy but
there is still so much more

of the show

to go.

Jackson has to sing the *mommies are people* part!

And "It's All Right to Cry" is coming up!

And "Girl Land"!

And "Don't Dress Your Cat in an Apron"!

With a real cat, in a real apron.

And suddenly I don't ever want it to end.

Any of it.

Finale

I look out at my brother
during "Sisters and Brothers."
My brother who is rolling his eyes, which I know is an
inside-joke thing
because it is our way of understanding each other,
from the inside out,
the way we make fun of things.
The way we give each other bloody knuckles
and headphones filled with old music.
The way I let him tell me what to make fun of and
what to take seriously.
The way he protects me.
Ain't we lucky.
Then Fiona and Sara and some other girls from the

Candy Land party do a dance while we all sing
"Glad to Have a Friend Like You."
This is where I get to say a few lines on my own.
Where I get to sing-act.
This was my original big part, the one I worked on
with Elana.
The one where I get to say *ooey-gooey*
and *sticky-licky*
and *fair and fun and skippin' free.*
I look right at Quinn when I say my lines, because she
helps me think about
the people I'm glad to have instead of the ones
I'm glad not to have.
At long last and extra loud because this is it,
we sing "Free to Be . . . You and Me."
The finale,
the end.
And when it's over, and we're all free to be ourselves
again,
free to go out into the audience and
hug Mom and Dad,
I think that I have one thing I don't hate
about Stephanie.

She's here.

She got my dad here, and there is no boil in him,

no simmer, even.

Warm, though.

Tickling and cheerful.

I could never do that on my own.

My mom hugs me and she and my dad nod at each

other and he says

This is Stephanie.

Can you believe they still do this show? Mom says,

shaking Stephanie's hand.

Well, they did all right by it, Dad says, squeezing my

shoulders with both of his hands.

Especially you, Stephanie says to me.

You really did, babe, Mom says.

Then she says

Was that James I saw?

I just shrug. *Couldn't be,* I say.

Voice Mail

I forgot to tell you something, I say
after I dial Quinn's home phone number.
I went through my backpack
to clean it out since Mom said she
CANNOT take another disgusting backpack clean-out
herself.
I found a lot of things—
a foldout ruler,
hot-purple Post-its,
Quinn's phone number,
which she had scribbled down after we won the
marshmallow-and-pretzel-stick contest,
no thanks to motormouth.
School supplies.

These things at the bottom of my bag—
mixed in with the crumbs of birthday cookies,
some rocks I found on the playground—
things for next year,
can be rinsed off like new.
And then the acrostic, the reason for my call,
folded up like the ruler,
but in a triangle.
I read it to Quinn now—
How had I forgotten to tell her about it?
All this time.
So many things happened in between.
We should write one ourselves, she says
right after she says *NO WAY Jackson wrote that.*
He's too good at spelling.
But do you think he thinks you're pretty? she asks.
Ew, no, I say.
And we spend a lot of time hanging out on the phone,
laughing at funny ideas for an acrostic called
FOUR ANNOYING BOYS.
Will take a lot of time and collaboration
to get through all those letters.

All summer maybe.
We'll save it all up—our ideas, our notes,
our acrostic—
like the leftover school supplies—
make things shiny and new
for next year.

End-of-Year Picnic

Mom, who couldn't make it to the Thanksgiving feast,
always makes it to the picnic.
She likes fresh air and new seasons.
We are outside on blankets and there are watermelons
and Popsicles and picnic lunches.
I sit with Quinn and eat a turkey sandwich while she
eats peanut butter with Marshmallow Fluff, a
special treat because we are outside.
The only allergies out here are flowers and grass
and bees
and there's no escaping any of that.
We get up and climb the monkey bars and I watch as
Mom and Quinn's mom
chitchat.

Maybe about the weather or work or the flu or maybe divorce

or maybe cancer.

Maybe they will be friends now and have lunch

the way some moms do,

talk to each other on the phone,

plan more playdates for us.

Plot together about getting us into the same class again next year.

After the summer,

when the mail truck arrives,

when the butterflies arrive.

When a whole new school year stretches out and we are far away from this one.

When it won't matter

what the room assignment card says,

because I have Quinn,

no matter what.

We are best friends,

we decided

on top of the monkey bars,

while the moms chitchatted,

while the FOUR ANNOYING BOYS

played ball.
While Fiona and Sara danced
a routine
under a tree.
While we ate watermelon Jelly Bellys that once rolled
across the kitchen floor.
Her birthday is September third,
just the right time of year to shop for
school supplies,
to start writing things down
in her *Stargirl* journal.
Best friends forever.

Small Moments

I carry a box out to James on the last day,
where there is shouting and picture taking and moms
shaking their heads because
where did the year go
and where it smells like
summer.
Jeez, what's all this? he asks.
It's my stuff from the year, I say.
My work.
My teacher, who looks old but who is just gray,
and who never did yell,
not even when I fell off my chair laughing,
who would never say *mathathon,*
but who knows how to teach math,
has been the best teacher I have ever had.

Attached to everyone's box was a note from Mrs. Soto.
I read mine right away.
She said she liked my way with words.
Pretty voice with pretty things to say, she wrote.
She said I have a gift.
Said I notice a lot of things other people miss.
She said it is the small moments that fill up our
big lives.
She said it's worth writing down.
Don't worry, I say to James.
It's my stuff.
I'll carry it.

acknowledgments

"Glad to Have a Friend Like You" from *Free to Be . . . You and Me* had lots to do with the writing of this book—it not only reminds me of my first-grade classroom, where it was the background music to many an arts-and-crafts project, but captures for me exactly what it feels like to have meaningful and lasting childhood friendships. I thank my dear friend Rhonda Penn Seidman—who has been showing me since we were two years old how friendship is done. And I thank the incredible friends I've made in my adult life, whose stories are interesting and wonderful and who make me laugh and who make it easier to be a good mother and a good writer.

Thanks also to the incredible teachers and staff at Manorhaven Elementary. Laurey Brevig-Almirall,

Lynette O'Brien, Joe Lennon, Alyssa Zendzian, Lorraine Bellman, Stephanie Seidner, Jennifer Kim, and Lourdes Perez, you inspire my kids and me every single day. Thanks also to one of a kind librarian, Maryellen Noone, to Principal Bonni Cohen, and to Margaret Kujan who has always managed to make special some of the smallest moments of them all.

As in fiction, sometimes life comes full circle in the most surprising and wonderful ways. I'm so grateful for Michelle Nagler, whose insights and loving care of this book have made it better and, more than anything, the book I always wanted it to be. Thanks also to everyone else at Random House Children's Books who left their mark on this book, especially Caroline Abbey and Leslie Mechanic, and to the incredible Julie Morstad, whose jacket artwork brought this book to life all at once, making beautiful the nervous butterflies that flit around inside us.

Thanks, Jill Grinberg, for believing in my work and in me from the start and when I most certainly did not. I am grateful beyond words.

Thank you, Gail Levine, for being my mom, for bringing light and love and side-splitting laughs to the not-always-brightly-lit spaces of childhood. Thanks to my dad, Charles Levine, for putting the top down and blasting the Weavers and for letting me sit in the jump seat on our nights with you.

Thanks to Michael Levine, to whom this book is dedicated, for letting me be in the room, most of the time. Every girl should have a big brother like you— for the grit, the wicked sense of humor, and the much cooler taste in music.

Thanks to my extended Ain family, whose constant support makes me feel especially blessed.

Thank you to Jon Ain, who reads my pages over and over, even if I've only changed two words. You are the realest, and I love you through and through.

And to my kiddos, exceptional in ways I could not possibly think up on my own, Grace and Elijah, who let me eavesdrop on their lives more than they should have to. I'm hoping this time around, you get a little glimpse into mine. Love you both to the moon and back.

beth ain

grew up in Allentown, Pennsylvania, where she and her best friend were free to finger-paint in the basement, and make plays, and get in and out of fights and hysterical fits of laughter, all to the soundtrack of *Free to Be . . . You and Me.* She is glad to have friends and family who encouraged her to be creative with her memories. She is the author of several books for children, including the Starring Jules series. She lives in Port Washington, New York, with her husband and two children. Visit her online at bethain.com.